MIKE WILKS

Holt, Rinehart and Winston   New York

To the memory of John Knowler

Text and illustrations Copyright © 1983 by Mike Wilks

All rights reserved, including the right to reproduce
this book or portions thereof in any form.
Published by Holt, Rinehart and Winston,
383 Madison Avenue, New York, New York 10017.
Published simultaneously in Canada by Holt, Rinehart
and Winston of Canada, Limited.

Library of Congress Cataloging in Publication Data
Wilks, Mike.
The weather works.
Summary: A vast and sprawling factory churns out
weather in all its variations.
[1. Stories in rhyme. 2. Weather—Fiction] I. Title.
PZ8.3.W667We 1983 [Fic] 82-23306
ISBN 0-03-59591-6

First Edition

Designer: Mike Wilks
Printed and bound by Mandarin International, Ltd., Hong Kong.
1 3 5 7 9 10 8 6 4 2

ave you noticed that lately the weather's gone mad?
It couldn't get very much worse.
You're entitled to know just why it's this bad
So I've set down the reason in verse.

Look up at a star, it's incredibly far
But farther away altogether,
Set off past the rainbow, bear due east at Mars,
Then sharp left soon after forever.

Bathed in cold starlight of jasper and jade,
In that faraway region there lurks
A vast rumbling factory where weather is made;
They call it the great Weather Works.

High vaulted glass ceilings arch over the floors.
The halls are so long and so wide
That huge as it seems from outside the front doors
It's very much larger inside.

In charge of the Works is the Big Man himself–
In all weather matters he's boss.
Though he started the business to bring in great wealth,
The fact is he makes quite a loss.

Inside the great factory almost every day
The visiting tourist may wish
To take the Great Tour: you just step up and pay
For your ticket, a marzipan fish.

From his mock-tudor cottage up high on a vat
The guide briskly came down the stairs
To a visiting party that quietly sat
Clasping sticky green marzipan fares.

"There's one rule by which all our guests must abide:
KEEP YOUR PETS UNDER STRICTEST CONTROL.
Don't let them run off, keep them right at your side
Every step of the way as we stroll."

There to his distress skulked an ominous mess.
On a leash–but quite loathsome and fey.
Though the guide flashed a smile I would have to confess
That his mood became suddenly grey.

They started the tour as the guide said "Now let's..."
(As I say he was feeling quite low
And was keeping an eye on the troublesome pet)
"...begin where we make all the snow."

On that hallway there's always a nip in the air.
Getting chilblains or frostbite is easy.
The tourists were glad that their toes were not bare
But the guide felt increasingly queasy.

While leading the party out into the frost
His worries refused to recede–
What if this strange creature should somehow get lost
And commit some great dastardly deed?

In this chamber the snow is concocted each night
And new frost is hatched without heat.
A high-ranking sailor made such a fine sight
As he stood there reviewing the sleet.

The party observing the wonders of cold,
All the acres of whiteness sublime,
Didn't notice their worried young guide growing old
As his hair turned the colour of lime.

The party enchanted (the guide quite afraid)
Moved into the blazing hot hall
Where the sunshine and sunbeams and dry winds are made
In great furnaces twenty feet tall.

There are rivers of sun (like lava that flows)
In deep channels, cooled slightly by fans.
The workers all wear tropic headgear and clothes
And of course have perpetual tans.

The place is so hot that it has a mirage
Reflected from heaven-knows-where,
Of elephants, memsahibs, the whole British Raj,
And a shimmering view of Red Square.

There in the heat perspiration was flowing
The tourists were standing too near
To those vats where the hot liquid sunshine was glowing
(Yet the guide's sweat was brought on by fear).

he group came to a halt when they saw RAINBOW HALL
The colours above were so bright
Souvenirs of the tour were there purchased by all
So they wouldn't forget the fine sight.

Fresh rainbows, transparent and perfect in hue,
Glowed above, with no colour deleted:
Red, orange, and yellow, green, violet, and blue,
And indigo–freshly completed.

Strikes there are rife–it is their way of life–
They fight over matters inane.
So rainbows, held up by industrial strife,
Quite rarely appear with the rain.

The guide was now older, his hair long and grey.
His beard was halfway to his thighs.
Shop stewards could see he was ageing away
With a woebegone look in his eyes.

High on a causeway the group paused to stare
Looking out across great bubbling tanks
Where billowing clouds were cooked up with great care,
Then numbered and ordered in banks.

This room is filled up with deep silence, profound.
Mere "quiet" is too small a word.
The mightiest shout there would not make a sound.
Explosions would hardly be heard.

There were cleaners at work using brushes of silk
To sweep out the cloud-brewing vats.
The sludge at the bottom is pure malted milk–
Which the workers take home to their cats.

The group gladly took in this vista so fine
Till the guide urged them all to depart
For the strange pet was quiet (a dangerous sign)
And the guide feared that mayhem would start.

The poor guide took his charges to QUALITY HALL
Where control engineers analyze
Every piece of new weather, no matter how small,
So it's perfect when dropped to the skies.

"A fast wind must blow in gusts gusting just so.
Morning sun must be just the right heat.
And not only are there seven sizes of snow,
But we also make four kinds of sleet."

As he gave this fine tour to the party he led,
The guide was quite weary at heart.
He looked to the very next portion with dread
For he feared *there* the trouble would start.

Though the guide just that morning had seemed a fine man
Not a year more than thirty and eight,
Now he looked pained and aged as only one can
Who's been dealt such a cruel hand by fate.

And now the guide tightened right up like a fist
As they walked–his whole mind was agog.
They'd come to the mill where they brew all the mist
And weave dark leaden blankets of fog.

They entered the mill–visibility nil
And the group quickly vanished from sight
In the swirling grey cloud of dampness and chill
(Though the guide could see clearly *his* plight).

He finally emerged from that darkness like night
And the moisture ran down from his hair.
As he counted each head as it came into sight
He discovered the pet wasn't there!

The guide started to twitch and developed an itch
On the uppermost side of his brain,
And a whine of high pitch from his ear issued which
Was the sound of one driven insane.

He foamed and boiled over–his mind became wild
He knew madness and all that's beyond.
He jumped up and down like a maniac child
Shouting "Whippets!" and "Burn down the pond!"

While the guide shouted on at a furious pace
Through his froth (to the tune of some hymns)
That vile pet was sneakily seeking a place
To act out its grimmest of whims.

It ran to The Office and bolted right in.
There are ten thousand desks in that spot.
Clerks file ninety forms for each storm they begin–
You think weather's easy? *It's not!*

It's tea break at ten and then once again
At twelve, but at twenty past two,
To refresh the brain there's a cup of warm rain,
Or a mug full of rain-flavoured dew.

As the beast scurried past people cried out, aghast,
And looked up from their paperwork chores.
But before they could grab it, that pet, oh so fast,
Had darted on out through the doors.

That pet ran to RESEARCH, the great secret section
Where bright weather ideas are worked through.
New brainstorms are tested and brought to perfection–
There's nothing that Research can't do.

Their plans for new weather are largely complete.
They know all about ratio and size,
And their pneumatic sunbeams and digital sleet
Will soon be sent into the skies.

The pet went on past to the place that it sought:
A red room labelled clearly: DISASTERS
And proceeded to do just what it ought not
(Like all mischievous beasts who've no masters).

Red buttons arrayed with instructions conveyed
In bold words most alarming to read,
That when pushed and played a vast nightmare parade
Would begin…The pet pressed with all speed.

From deep down in the Works rose a great metal cry
As machinery started to groan.
It shuddered and quivered and screeched to the sky
Causing terrified workers to moan.

The great Lightning Chamber went lightning-berserk
And the Thunder Hall rumbled and boomed
And the poor storm technicians were driven from work
And in fear felt they somehow were doomed.

From the Tunnel of Winds monster cyclones spun out
And the storm raged with wild random force.
'Twas the worst weather *ever*, of that there's no doubt–
And all caused by that one pet, of course.

The rain fell in torrents–it poured out a zoo.
It rained badgers, not just cats and dogs.
Down came ferrets and pythons and stoats and a shrew,
And then thousands and thousands of frogs.

That storm would have raged till the Works was drained dry
But alarm bells went off and connected
To a siren, which wailed an incredible cry–
Every ear in the place was affected.

The Big Man himself, made aware by this pitch,
To his desk firmly strode with a frown.
He calmly reached out for the great master switch
And shut the whole Weather Works down.

All the weather was cancelled and silence descended
Up and down the entire shop floor.
Everyone was relieved the disaster had ended
And order prevailed there once more.

The culprit was sought and eventually caught
And was straightaway hauled into court.
The jury, distraught to learn what had been wrought,
Heard a grim and disturbing report.

The indictment was read to that obnoxious pest.
The grim scene brought a tear to each eye.
The pet was hardpressed and it finally confessed
While its master sat glumly nearby.

They sentenced that pet–sent it far, far away–
But the damage it caused was still there,
For the man it drove mad on that terrible day
Was still howling and pulling his hair.

That poor old guide's illness grew so out of scale
'Twas too big for his head altogether.
It burst forth from his mind in the form of a whale
Which swam right out into the weather.

The Big Man knew well a good vessel was needed
To follow and catch this odd whale.
So he hired the PEQUOD, a ship that proceeded
To steam through the Works on its trail.

They hunted that spectre with hook and harpoon
Till everything pointed was spent.
They started at noon on the nineteenth of June
With no sign of success by next Lent.

They fastened a chain to a heavyweight spanner
And over and over they'd cast
At the whale, which swam 'round in an adamant manner–
They vowed they would get it at last.

But each throw that missed fell down into the Works
And they'd haul it back up by its chain
Inflicting great damage, in spasms and jerks–
And it happened again and again.

We've seen the strange outcome all over the land–
For year after year we have had
Odd weather that just seems to get out of hand
And seasons that truly seem mad.

So watch what *you* do, wheresoever you roam,
And *please* don't you ever forget:
When you venture abroad, or in your own home,
Keep strictest control of your pet.

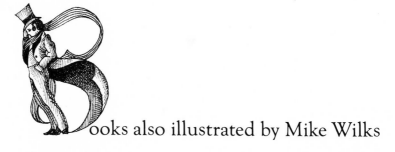ooks also illustrated by Mike Wilks

PILE – Petals from St. Klaed's Computer
Text by Brian W. Aldiss

In Granny's Garden
Text by Sarah Harrison